D0459409

For Emma Tsenti ~ J.W.

To Wendy ~ T.R.

First published in Great Britain in 2012 by Andersen Press Ltd.,
20 Vauxhall Bridge Road, London SW1V 2SA.
Published in Australia by Random House Australia Pty.,
Level 3, 100 Pacific Highway, North Sydney, NSW 2060.
Text copyright © Jeanne Willis, 2012
Illustration copyright © Tony Ross, 2012
The rights of Jeanne Willis and Tony Ross to be identified
as the author and illustrator of this work have been
asserted by them in accordance with the
Copyright, Designs and Patents Act, 1988.
All rights reserved.
Colour separated in Switzerland by Photolitho AG, Zürich.
Printed and bound in Singapore by Tien Wah Press.
Tony Ross has used pastels in this book.

10   9   8   7   6   5   4   3   2   1

British Library Cataloguing in Publication Data available.
ISBN 978 1 84939 344 7
This book has been printed on acid-free paper

Fly, Chick, Fly!

Jeanne Willis   Tony Ross

ANDERSEN PRESS

In the middle of the wood, there was an oak tree.

In the middle of the oak tree, there was a hole.

In the middle of the hole, there was a nest.

In the middle of the nest, there were three eggs.

In the middle of the eggs, there was an owl . . .

She sat on the eggs all day and night.

For thirty days and nights.

Every dawn, every dusk, Father Owl went
hunting to feed Mother Owl.

When the blossom was in bud, the first chick hatched.

When the blossom was open, the second chick hatched.

When the blossom fell, the third chick hatched.

Ten times a day, Father Owl went hunting.
Ten times a day, Mother Owl fed the chicks.

The chicks grew and grew.

When the blackberries were green,
the first chick tried to fly.
She flapped. She flipped. She flopped . . .
But then she flew!

When the blackberries were ripe,
the second chick tried to fly.
He flapped. He flipped. He flopped . . .
Then he flew too!

The blackberries had gone.

The leaves were turning brown.

But the last chick was still in the nest.

"Fly!" said Mother Owl.

"Not I!" said the last chick.

She would not even try.

"You
must fly!"
said her mother.
"You must fly!"
said her father.

"Why?" said the last chick.

"If I fly, the crow might get me.
If I fly, the rain might wet me.
If I fly, a train might hit me.
My sister flew and never came back.
Why would I want to fly?"

"You belong in the sky," said her mother.
"Your sister is at home in the old elm tree.
Fly, little chick, just try!"

The last chick clung to the end of a branch.
She flapped. She flipped. She flopped . . .

. . . and hopped back into the nest.

"Time to go," said Father Owl.
But the last little chick cried, "No, no, no!
My brother flew and never came back.
Was he eaten by a crow or killed on the track?
Why would I want to fly?"

"You belong in the sky," said her father.
"Your brother is at home in the old birch tree.
Fly, little chick, just try!"

So the last chick left the nest.
She crept to the end of the branch.
She flapped. She flipped. She flopped.
And this time . . .

She flew!

Snow came. Crow came. Spring came.
But what became of this last chick?

In the wood, there is a beech tree.

In the middle of the beech tree, there is a hole.

In the middle of the hole, there is a nest.

In the middle of the nest, there is an owl.

She was the last chick to fly.

But she is glad she flew because . . .

. . . here is *her* first chick!